CHARLOTTE MIDDLETON
presents

CHRISTOPHER Nibble

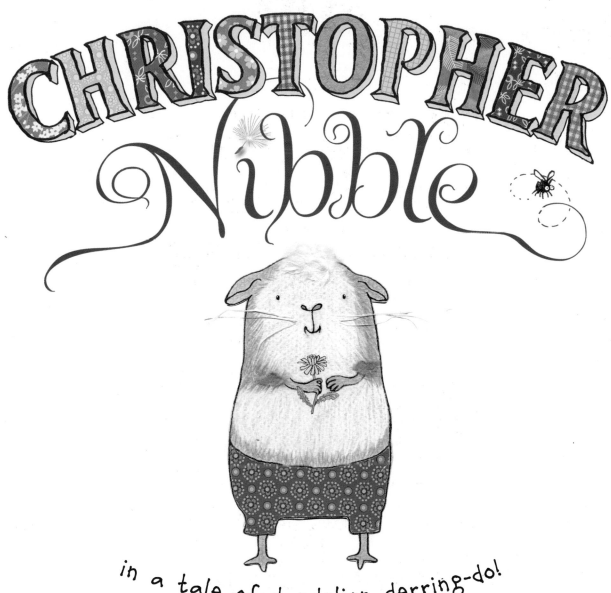

in a tale of dandelion derring-do!

OXFORD
UNIVERSITY PRESS

If there was one thing Christopher Nibble **loved** more than football,

it was . . .

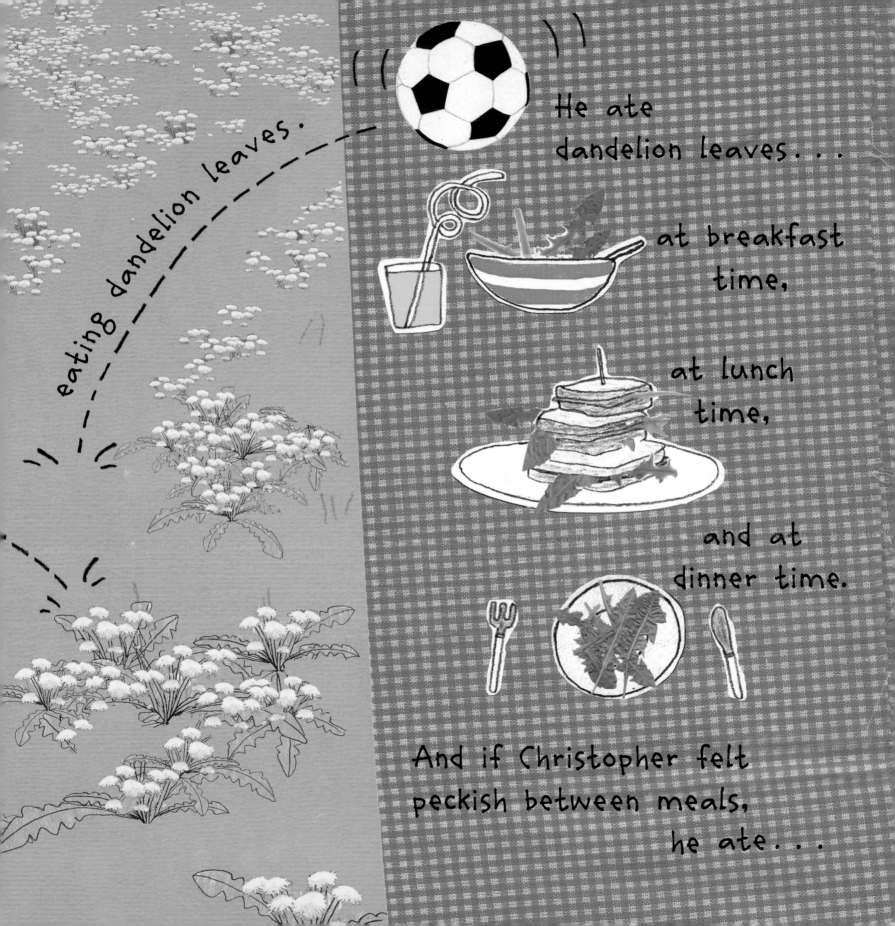

eating dandelion leaves.

He ate dandelion leaves...

at breakfast time,

at lunch time,

and at dinner time.

And if Christopher felt peckish between meals, he ate...

MORE dandelion leaves!
But it was not just Christopher who liked
dandelion leaves. Mr and Mrs Nibble liked them.
His sister liked them. His friends liked them.

For Betty and Jack, with fond memories.

Nicola and Charlotte

OXFORD
UNIVERSITY PRESS

Great Clarendon Street, Oxford OX2 6DP

Oxford University Press is a department of the University of Oxford.
It furthers the University's objective of excellence in research, scholarship,
and education by publishing worldwide in

Oxford   New York

Auckland   Cape Town   Dar es Salaam   Hong Kong   Karachi
Kuala Lumpur   Madrid   Melbourne   Mexico City   Nairobi
New Delhi   Shanghai   Taipei   Toronto

With offices in

Argentina   Austria   Brazil   Chile   Czech Republic   France   Greece
Guatemala   Hungary   Italy   Japan   Poland   Portugal   Singapore
South Korea   Switzerland   Thailand   Turkey   Ukraine   Vietnam

Oxford is a registered trade mark of Oxford University Press
in the UK and in certain other countries

British Library Cataloguing in Publication Data available

ISBN: 978-0-19-272865-4 (hardback)
ISBN: 978-0-19-272866-1 (paperback)

2 4 6 8 10 9 7 5 3 1

Printed in China

Paper used in the production of this book is a natural,
recyclable product made from wood grown in sustainable forests.
The manufacturing process conforms to the environmental
regulations of the country of origin

In fact. . . every guinea pig
in Dandeville **loved** dandelion leaves.

munch

munch

nibble

munch

nibble

All day long the happy
sound of munching and
nibbling filled the air. . .

until, that is, dandelion leaves began to run out.

Dandelion dishes were taken off the menus, and dandelion drinks disappeared from the shelves.

Menu Today

Carrot and lettuce wrap on a bed of ~~dandelion~~ leaves
cabbage

~~Dandelion~~ soup
cabbage

cabbage
~~Dandelion~~ and broccoli quiche

~~Dandelion~~
~~juice~~ sold out

The last few leaves could be bought
on the internet...

for a HUGE amount of money!

with chewy cabbage instead!

Just one dandelion was left but nobody knew about it, except Christopher Nibble. It happened to be growing right outside his bedroom window.

Christopher's mouth
watered at the sight of it.
But he knew he mustn't eat it,
or let anyone else eat it,
not if it was the last dandelion in town.

It might even be the last dandelion
in the whole world!
He thought hard and decided. . .

... to go to
the library.

Cookery

MONTY POIS

The Oriental Cabbage

NIBBLE'S CHRISTMAS

PRIDE & POISSON

DAN DE LÉON

GORDON RHUBARB

101 Lettuce Recipes

Hollyhock Magic!

Pippi Parsnip

CHEESE PLEASE

JAMIE CAULIFLOWER

THE VERY HUNGRY GRUB

Ready, Steady, Nibble

WAR @ PIZZA

Sports

The Tour de Dandeville

MINI GOLF

MARATHON MOUSE

FOOTBALL MAD

SOCCER

CYCLING FOR GERBILS

Flowers   Weeds

Dandelions

Cloche Gardening

Shoots, Leaves & Weeds

The LAWN EATING EXPERT

Brassica Breeding

WEEDS

THE VERY HUNGRY GUINEA PIG

Bugs

He borrowed a book called
'Everything You Need to
Know about Dandelions'

and he read it very carefully.

He found a little cloche to protect his dandelion. . .

and every day he watered it and picked off the bugs.

Every day he was very good about not taking even the tiniest little nibble while he . . .

waited,
and waited,
and waited.

Until, finally, his dandelion had grown the most beautiful white head of tiny seeds.

Very gently,
Christopher picked it
and carried it all
the way up
Daisy Chain Hill.
When he reached
the top. . .

he had just
enough puff to take
a deep breath and. . .

The seeds filled the air...

and landed gently all over Dandeville.

At first nobody noticed.

But soon the new
plants started to sprout
fresh leaves.

And in no time at all Dandeville
was filled with the happy sound
of munching once more.

As for Christopher,

But now

there's

something

he loves just

as much

as eating

dandelions . . . .

Christopher loves **GROWING** them!